Lucy's Badger Cub

Mary has been writing books for children and teenagers for fifteen years, and has now had more than 50 titles published. She writes funny stories, animal stories, spooky stories and romantic stories, and before she started *Lucy's Farm* she spent some time in Devon to be sure she got all the details right. Mary has two grown-up children and lives just outside London in a small Victorian cottage. She has a cat called Maisie and a collection of china rabbits. She says her favourite hobby is "pottering", as this is when she gets most of her ideas.

All of LUCY'S FARM books can be ordered at your local bookshop or are available by post from Book Service by Post (tel: 01624 675137).

LUCY'S FARM

Lucy's Badger Cub

Mary Hooper

Illustrations by Anthony Lewis

MACMILLAN CHILDREN'S BOOKS

First published 2000 by Macmillan Children's Books
a division of Macmillan Publishers Limited
25 Eccleston Place, London SW1W 9NF
Basingstoke and Oxford
www.macmillan.co.uk

Associated companies throughout the world

ISBN 0 330 36796 X

Text copyright © Mary Hooper 2000
Illustrations copyright © Anthony Lewis 2000

1 3 5 7 9 8 6 4 2

A CIP catalogue record for this book is available from
the British Library

Phototypeset by Intype London Ltd
Printed and bound in Great Britain by Mackays of Chatham plc, Kent

Chapter One

"There," Lucy whispered, nodding towards the grassy, bluebell-covered bank. "Just over there. I'm sure I can see something moving."

Bethany frowned. "I can't see a thing!"

"You're looking the wrong way. *There!*" Lucy's voice rose excitedly. "Here he comes. I can see a black-and-white snout. I can see his two little ears!"

It was dusk, and Lucy Tremayne and her best friend Bethany Brown were flat on their tummies behind a bush in Brockham Woods, near Hollybrook Farm, where Lucy lived with her mum, dad and little sister Kerry.

The Tremaynes' farm had a herd of black-and-white Friesian cows and a small flock of sheep which included Rosie, a lamb Lucy had bottle-fed since she was an hour old. There was also Donald, a donkey Lucy had rescued from the beach, the two farm dogs – Roger and Podger – a clutch of chickens and a handful of cats. Lucy loved animals!

"Oh, I see him!" Beth said suddenly. "Isn't he huge!"

"Enormous!" Lucy said, for the big badger rustling in the undergrowth was nearly a metre long and very broad.

"He must be one of the top dogs," Lucy said, and then giggled. "I mean top badgers. Boars, Mrs Fern called them."

The two girls both went to the local school in Bransley, which was a village in the Devon countryside a mile from the sea. Mrs Fern, their teacher, had been doing a project on wild animals, with special emphasis on badgers because of all the setts – the underground tunnels where badgers lived – which lay around the village.

"Mrs Fern said that badgers use those setts for years. Sometimes for a hundred years!" Beth said.

Lucy watched spellbound at the sight before her, twisting a lock of blonde hair round and round her finger. "Look! There's more of them appearing!" she whispered.

"And one of them is bringing out the dirty straw bedding!" Beth said. "Just like Mrs Fern told us."

Lucy nodded. "She said they line their nest chambers with dry grass and straw which they change quite often."

"And that some *very* clean ones will make loos for themselves above ground!" Beth marvelled. She paused. "D'you think they've got any babies? D'you think they'll bring them out so we can see them?"

"I think the cubs are born in January or February, but don't come out into the daylight until they're about eight weeks old, when it's a bit warmer," Lucy said. She counted on her fingers. "That's about now, so if we come here regularly we might see them."

"I'd love to see *babies*," Beth said longingly.

Both girls watched breathlessly as the badgers went about their evening business – cleaning out their burrows, fetching new bedding, foraging for food and snuffling in the undergrowth. Some of the younger, smaller ones seemed to be playing fighting games with each other.

After a while Lucy looked at her watch. "We ought to be getting back," she said reluctantly. "It's nearly seven o'clock and it'll be getting dark soon." As she spoke, a soft mist was already rising from the damp earth and a dusky greyness was coming over the woods. The birds which had been twittering overhead fell silent as they roosted in the trees.

Beth's jaw dropped. "I didn't realize it was so late! I'm supposed to be home by seven!"

"We'll cut across the fields to your house," Lucy said. "It'll only take a few minutes."

The instant the girls got to their feet and began to brush themselves down, all the badgers disappeared, vanishing back into their setts.

"Shame!" Lucy said. "But now we know where they are, we can come again."

"I bet Courtney would like to come and see them too," Beth said as they set off along the path through the trees.

Lucy wrinkled her nose. She wasn't too keen on Courtney, who'd only recently come to live in the village. Lucy and Beth had been best friends since they'd been babies, but now Courtney was around it wasn't quite the same. Sometimes it seemed to Lucy that Courtney was trying to take Beth away from her. The other annoying thing about Courtney was that she never stopped going on about London, where she'd lived before, telling them how exciting it was there. Courtney, of course, thought Bransley was boring.

"I didn't think Courtney liked animals much," Lucy said now.

"It's cows and stuff she doesn't like," Beth explained. "I'm sure she'd be interested in badgers."

Lucy shrugged. "She can come if she wants to."

"Don't sound so keen!" Beth said, and Lucy grinned at her friend.

Walking back, Lucy soon forgot about Courtney. She *loved* the woods, especially at dusk when there was a soft, almost unearthly, light. Above was the thick green shade of a million fresh new leaves and beneath was the lush, damp smell of bracken, fallen leaves and fungi. At this time of the year it was extra special because of the soft violet haze and musky scent given off by hundreds of bluebells.

"When did someone last live *there*?" Beth said suddenly, nodding at the deserted, tumbledown cottage they were just approaching.

Lucy shook her head. "I don't know.

Dad told me that years and years ago it belonged to a woodman."

"Looks pretty spooky," Beth said.

Lucy nodded and lowered her voice. "Dad *said* it was a woodman, but I think a witch lived there!"

Beth laughed nervously. "Don't be daft."

"A witch with a black cat," Lucy said huskily. "And every night at midnight the witch would go out on her broomstick to frighten the people in the village. Sometimes she'd take small children away with her and they'd never be seen again."

Beth gave a short scream. "Stop! I don't want to hear any more." She paused by the fence. "We go across that stile and through the field here, don't we?"

Lucy nodded. "But hang on a moment. I want to look through the windows of that cottage."

"No, don't!"

"I just want to see if there's anything inside . . ."

Before Beth could stop her, Lucy was making her way towards the cottage, kicking through the blackberry bushes and thick nettles along what had once been the garden path.

The cottage was tiny, two windows down and two up, with a grey slate roof and funny lopsided chimney. The walls were made of crumbling stone and plaster and you could hardly see the door because it was completely covered with clambering dark ivy and brambles.

"Oh, hurry up!" Beth called.

Lucy pulled at one of the ivy strands which covered the nearest window and rubbed at the grimy glass. She didn't know what she expected to see – funny old furniture covered in dust, perhaps, or a pile of musty books. What she saw, though, was a small, shiny camping stove, right in the middle of the sitting room floor. With a kettle on it.

"Oh!" she said.

"What? Hurry up!" Beth said as Lucy made her way back down the path.

"What did you see, then?" Beth asked as they hurried across the field.

Lucy was frowning, still trying to puzzle it out. "A cooking stove," she said. "Someone must be living there."

"Oh yes?" Beth said, grinning. "The witch, I suppose. And she's got the stove so she can cook herself a tasty frog supper."

Lucy shook her head. "Witches have

cauldrons," she said. "There's a real person living there."

But Beth just laughed, thinking Lucy was still joking.

The two girls crossed the field, walked down a lane and came to the village war memorial, where they parted company.

Still deep in thought, Lucy walked down Embrook Lane towards Hollybrook Farm, passing the big steel barn where their cows lived during the winter months. Climbing the gate which led into the farmyard, she crossed the yard and banged on the kitchen window to tell her mum she was back.

"We saw badgers! Loads of them!" she called.

Julie Tremayne, who was standing by the sink, nodded and smiled through the window. "That's nice!" she called back. She was a tall, pretty woman with blonde hair caught up on top of her head.

"I'll tell you more in a minute. I'm just going to check on the animals," Lucy said. She made her way down to the small paddock just along the lane from the farmyard and leaned over the gate. It was getting quite dark now but she could see the white furriness of the sheep's coats all in a huddle at the bottom of the paddock.

"Rosie!" Lucy called. "Come on, Rosie!"

A small white shape detached itself from the others and came galloping towards her, baa-ing loudly.

Lucy, laughing, leaned over the gate to scratch Rosie's nose. "Hello, lovely girl," she said. As a darker shape moved away from the hedge and began to come towards her, she added, "And hello, Donald! Couldn't forget you, could I?"

Lucy patted the head of her rescued donkey and he gave a loud bray which startled the sheep and made them all start bleating. Lucy laughed again. "Good-night to you, too," she called, and then she made her way back to the farmhouse to tell her mum and dad all about the badgers.

Chapter Two

The next day was Saturday, so Lucy was up earlier than usual. She liked to help her dad with the cows when she could – especially when there were new calves around. Teaching them to drink milk from a bucket instead of from a mother cow was one of Lucy's favourite jobs.

There were two calves that morning. Lucy had to get a bucket of fresh, creamy milk, dip her hand into it and try and get the calves to suck the milk from her fingers. Once they were doing this, she gradually moved her hand into the bucket until they were gulping up the milk for themselves.

It took a lot of patience, but by the time her dad had finished milking the rest of the herd, she'd got both new calves drinking from the bucket pretty well.

"Are we going back for breakfast now?" she asked her dad. "I'm starving!"

"Can you wait half an hour?" Tim Tremayne said. He was a tall man with gingery-fair hair, who looked tanned whatever time of the year it was.

Lucy nodded. "If I have to. What d'you want me to do, then?"

Her dad whistled to the two dogs who were lying by the entrance to the cow shed ready to nip at the heels of any cow who tried to escape. "If you go and get Kerry and your mum," he said, "we're going to drive the cows down to the summer field."

"Fantastic!" Lucy said, remembering the previous year.

The herd of Friesians that the Tremaynes owned spent most of the year in the big steel barn across the road from Hollybrook

Farm. They were fed and watered there, and went into the milking parlour next to the barn twice a day to be milked.

Once the weather was warmer, though, the cows went down the lane straight after milking in the morning, spent all day in a field eating juicy spring grass and were driven back to the parlour in time for afternoon milking. Once they got used to going to the field as part of their daily routine, Lucy's dad could manage them quite well on his own – with the help of Roger and Podger, of course. But the first time they went to the field every year all the family joined in to drive them down and watch the fun.

Ten minutes later, the cows meandered slowly and ponderously down the lane, driven onward by the dogs and by Lucy and her mum and dad. Even Kerry, lifted high by her mum, helped by shouting, "Go, Cow!" as loudly as she could.

Once they went through the five-bar gate into the big field, a change came over the herd. For some of them this was their first spring and the very first time they'd been let out to do as they pleased. Even for the older, more sedate cows, the idea of freedom – space, fresh air and as much grass and clover as they could eat – was a delightful one. As the cows entered the field and realized they were actually outside, they trotted and mooed and leapt about, thoroughly enjoying their new quarters.

"Oh, look!" Lucy called, as one cow jumped high in the air.

"See that one race!" her mum called back, as another ran up and down the field like a racehorse.

Two more rolled on their backs and kicked their legs in the air, making everyone laugh. Lucy knew that the novelty would wear off in a day or so, but today the cows were having the time of their lives.

"Weren't they funny!" Lucy said half an hour later, as the family tucked into a pile of scrambled eggs from their own chickens and big, flat, field mushrooms.

"Funny cows jump good!" Kerry said.

Julie Tremayne smiled. "See how she's putting sentences together!"

"These are pretty good, too," Lucy's dad said, holding up a mushroom on a fork.

"Kerry and I found them yesterday," said Lucy's mum. "Or Kerry did, actually.

We were walking to the village when she saw them in a field."

"How long did it take you to get to the village?" Lucy asked, for Kerry had only just started walking and stopped to inspect every blade of grass, leaf, stone and daisy along the way.

"Hours and hours!" Lucy's mum said, glancing fondly at Kerry, who'd been put on the floor and whose bottom could be seen sticking out of the saucepan cupboard in the dresser.

As Lucy and her dad were clearing the plates away, and Lucy was telling everyone yet again how brilliant the badgers had been, the phone rang. Lucy's mum went to answer it. It was some time before she came back in the room.

"Guess who!" she said, tucking some strands of curly hair behind her ears.

"Someone for Bed and Breakfast?" Lucy guessed. To earn some extra money, Lucy's mum and dad took in paying guests. Sometimes they were people who were on business in Honley, their nearest big town, but more usually they were families – or people on their own – who just wanted a relaxing farm holiday.

Lucy's mum shook her head. "No, not Bed and Breakfast," she said. "*That* was Major Steddington."

Tim Tremayne immediately stood to attention and did a mock salute. "Stand up straight, everyone!"

"He's very nice!" Lucy's mum protested. "And he wants us to do him a big favour."

Lucy's dad pulled a surprised face.

"But what can we do for him, Mum?" Lucy asked. She knew that Major Steddington lived about two miles away, on the other side of Bransley. He was a wealthy man who owned a stud farm, where racehorses were bred and also trained.

"Well," Lucy's mum said, "apparently he's just taken delivery of a very nervous young racehorse. They think it's going to be a real champion – it's already won some big races."

"What's that got to do with us?" Tim Tremayne asked.

"I was just coming to that. He's looking for a companion for it." Julie Tremayne looked at Lucy. "You know they sometimes use a placid dog or an older pony to befriend a nervous horse?"

Lucy nodded.

"Well, they can use donkeys, too. Major Steddington's heard about Donald and wondered if we'd lend him to the stud for a few months – just until his new race-horse settles down."

"Oh!" Lucy said. She thought for a moment. "That might be quite nice for Donald, mightn't it? Would I be able to go up and see him at the stables?"

"Of course," her mum said. "The major said you could visit any time."

"Sounds a good idea to me," Lucy's dad said. "Let that donkey eat Major Steddington out of house and home instead of us."

"Dad!" Lucy said. She looked at him severely. "I know you don't mean it. I know you love Donald just as much as I do."

"I'll love him even more if someone else is feeding him!" Her dad grinned at her. "Only teasing, love. Donald will love it there. He'll have the best of everything –

it'll be like going on holiday. D'you know, those horses even have a swimming pool!"

There was a sudden cry from Kerry, and Lucy's mum bent to retrieve her from the cupboard. "Donald's your donkey, Lucy, so the decision is entirely yours. I told the major I'd pass his message on and let you think about it."

Lucy didn't take long to make up her mind. Later that morning, her mother phoned the major and, that afternoon, a shiny black horse transporter arrived at Hollybrook Farm. Donald, newly groomed for the occasion, was led into it.

"It's *very* nice to be asked – and it's only for a little while," Lucy said to Donald, tying him up in the back of the transporter. "And I'm coming up there with you to see you settled in."

Major Steddington's manager, Giles, a tall man wearing a battered Barbour jacket, was driving the transporter, and he filled Lucy in on what Donald's role would be.

"Mostly he'll just be a companion for Eclipse – that's the new racehorse," he explained. "Eclipse is very valuable but also extremely nervous. He needs a friendly animal to calm him down."

"I'm sure Donald will be good at that," Lucy said. "Nothing seems to fluster him. Two dogs and half a dozen sheep can run circles round him and he won't turn a hair."

"Just what we want," Giles said, smiling.

Lucy, sitting in the front of the transporter, leaned forward eagerly as they went through the huge white gates of Steddington Stud. She'd been dying to see over the high walls for ages.

The stud farm covered many acres and was modern and stylish, with white-painted buildings and a central courtyard with great tubs of red and white flowers everywhere. On top of the walls were three small steel cameras, turning this way and that as they recorded everything that went on around the yards.

Giles explained that behind the courtyard were the offices of the stud, and beyond those the sleeping quarters of the stablehands. To the right was a large, low, L-shaped building in which the horses had their individual stables. He parked the transporter and Lucy clambered out.

There were horses everywhere! Horses being walked around, taken for exercise, groomed, or just standing looking out of their stable doors. And such beautiful horses – slender, elegant and glossy, tossing their manes and pawing the ground with their dainty hooves.

Lucy looked all around her. "It's not how I thought it would be," she said. "It's not like any stables I've ever been to. And there are so many people about. Not like on our farm where there's only my mum and dad and me to look after all our cows."

"Well, racehorses are a *very* valuable commodity," Giles said crisply. "And safety and security are our main concern – hence all the staff. We're about to have a brand-new security alarm system installed next month." He opened the back of the transporter. "Now, if you'd just like to lead your – er, Donald, is it? – over to the end stable where Eclipse is kept . . ."

Lucy led Donald across to what was going to be his holiday home. It was clean, airy and whitewashed, and as large as Lucy's bedroom. A man wearing green dungarees was sweeping in fresh sawdust.

"We're OK now, Rob. You can make yourself useful elsewhere," Giles said rather dismissively, and the man shot off somewhere.

"Just look at this!" Lucy whispered to Donald, leading him into the immaculate stable.

At the back of the stable, pressed against the wall, was a beautiful chestnut stallion with a white diamond mark on his head. Seeing Giles and Lucy he whinnied, tossed his head and seemed to press further against the wall.

"Don't go too near Eclipse!" Giles warned Lucy. "I want to leave the two animals alone to get to know each other."

Lucy tethered Donald loosely to a ring in the wall and patted him. "Be good," she whispered. "Be nice to Eclipse and I'll come back and see you soon."

Donald nodded his head up and down and Lucy smiled. He'd understood every word – she was sure of it.

Chapter Three

"How's Donald enjoying his holiday up at the stud farm?" Beth asked Lucy the following Friday as they walked down to Brockham Woods. The sun was just disappearing over the hills behind them, and long shadows crept before them across the field.

"I think he loves it," Lucy said. "I went up yesterday to see him. And Eclipse – the racehorse he's supposed to be looking after – really likes having him there. Apparently it's calmed him down so much that the stablehands can actually groom him now. Before, he went mad if anyone went too close."

29

"I'd love to go in and see the horses," Beth said longingly. "Couldn't you take me along next time you go?"

Lucy pulled a face. "I'll ask. They're really funny about strangers, though. It's because the horses are worth so much. Thousands and thousands of pounds. Millions," she said vaguely. "And they're not all that friendly there. I've met Major Steddington and he's OK, but some of the others just make me feel I'm in the way. There's a stableman called Rob who really snapped at me yesterday when I tried to give Eclipse a mint."

Beth raised her eyebrows so that they disappeared into her long fringe. "Perhaps I won't go, then."

They walked through the woods, which were growing dim and dusky now, and began to speak in whispers as they neared the badger sett. Settling themselves behind their usual bush, they waited quietly for ten minutes or so. Then Lucy noticed something odd.

"There's no used bedding around," she said, puzzled. "The badgers can't have been doing their housekeeping. I wonder why? And look at their holes – a lot of them have been bunged up with earth or branches. How could that happen?"

Beth shrugged. "Don't know. We could ask Miss Fern."

"It's really odd," Lucy said. She was mystified – and worried for some reason that she couldn't quite explain. Something was wrong, but she didn't know what.

Another fifteen minutes went by, and then another. Beth yawned. "Perhaps they've gone away. Gone to live somewhere else."

"I don't think they do that," Lucy said. "But I don't think they're here. Not tonight, at any rate. We might as well go." She was just about to get to her feet when she noticed a small movement from the top of the bank, and heard a rustling of leaves. "Hang on! I think one's coming out!" she hissed to Beth.

Both girls went quiet, staring at the place where the rustling was coming from.

A black nose appeared, followed by a stripy face.

"It's a baby one!" Lucy breathed. "He's tiny."

The girls watched, spellbound, as the small badger inched its way forward and looked up and down, then from side to side. It seemed, the girls thought, rather lost. It wasn't foraging for food or changing its bedding, it was just looking around.

After three minutes or so, without even looking for food, it disappeared back into the hole.

"Oh!" Lucy sighed.

"Wasn't he lovely!" Beth said. "Wasn't he the sweetest thing? Why d'you think he was on his own, though?"

"I don't know," Lucy replied, and she shook her head worriedly. "I've got the address of a badger sanctuary somewhere, though, and I think I'll give them a ring."

The girls waited another fifteen minutes, just in case, but the little badger didn't come out again, and no others appeared either. As darkness was falling fast, they decided they'd come back and try again the next day.

As they made their way back through the gathering gloom, along the pathway towards the old cottage, Lucy remembered that she had a torch in her pocket. She took it out.

"Beth," she said, "I want to have a quick look in that cottage. I want to find out if someone's been living there."

Beth pulled a face. "You said it was a witch's cottage. I don't want to go in. It's really creepy."

"I was only kidding about that," Lucy grinned. "And we won't be long. We'll go straight in and straight out again. You can stay downstairs if you want."

By this time, Lucy was already making her way down the path towards the cottage. Beth stood for a while, frowning, but then decided she didn't want to miss out on an adventure, even if she *was* scared.

The front door of the cottage was crisscrossed with brambles and ivy, so Lucy began pushing her way round to the back, through the undergrowth. This looked fairly clear of briars, as if it had been used quite recently.

"See that?" Lucy said, pointing at the latch on the door. "No dust or dirt. That means someone's been using it."

"There you are, then," Beth said. "Isn't that all you wanted to know?"

Lucy grinned. "No," she said. "I want to know who's been here. And why."

She looked through the nearest window to make sure there was no one inside and then slowly, gingerly, lifted the latch and pushed open the back door.

Beth peered over Lucy's shoulder. "Yuck!" she exclaimed.

There was just one room downstairs, with a small kitchen leading off it. The main room was dark and damp, with piles of newspapers in the corner and a rotting chair in the middle of the floor. The fireplace was filled with ashes and burnt paper, and curtains hung in rags from the windows.

Lucy shone her torch around her, on the cobwebs hanging from the ceiling, the mould growing across the walls, and the spiders scuttling into corners.

"I thought you said there was a cooking stove here," Beth whispered.

"There was," Lucy said. "It's gone now. I bet they've hidden it."

"Maybe you imagined it," Beth said. "It doesn't look as if there's been anyone living here for years and years."

"I bet there has . . ." Lucy said.

While Beth stood nervously in the doorway, Lucy peered into the little kitchen. Not a trace of anyone! "Let's go upstairs," she said.

"Let's not!"

"I just want to see what's up there."

Lucy was already halfway up the rickety staircase by this time, so Beth reluctantly followed her.

"There might be treasure!" Lucy whispered.

"There might be spiders!" Beth replied fearfully.

There was an ancient bathroom upstairs and a bedroom which had no bed in it. There was, however, a rolled-up sleeping bag in a corner of the room.

"There!" Lucy flicked the torch over it triumphantly. "Look at that. There *is* someone sleeping here."

"OK," Beth said nervously. "So can we go now?"

"All right, I—" Lucy began, and then she stopped dead.

There was the sound of footsteps outside. Someone was coming along the path in the woods. *Someone was walking round to the back of the cottage.*

Beth gave a tiny scream. "It's the witch!" she said.

Lucy turned off her torch, and the shadows of the room closed about them so that they could no longer see into the dark corners. Outside, an owl hooted, making them both jump, and for a moment Lucy almost believed in the witch. Then she remembered she'd made it up. "Of course it's not a witch!" she muttered. She thought quickly. There was a big cupboard at the top of the staircase, and she opened this and pulled Beth in with her.

They weren't a moment too soon. Suddenly the back door opened and they heard someone come into the cottage with a heavy tread.

"Suppose they come upstairs!" Beth whispered in a terrified voice.

"Ssshh!"

Lucy held her breath, more nervous than she was letting on. It was pitch-black in the cupboard. It smelt fusty and stale and, she was quite sure, was home to a whole tribe of spiders, earwigs and beetles. She hoped they weren't going to have to stay there too long. More than that, she hoped whoever was downstairs wasn't going to come up!

They heard the footsteps go across the downstairs room and into the kitchen. A moment later they heard the same footsteps cross the room again, then the back door opened and shut. There was the sound of someone walking down the path.

"They've gone!" Lucy said thankfully, and she pushed open the cupboard door.

"That was awful," Beth said, sounding shaky. "I thought we were going to have to stay in there all night. I thought we'd suffocate."

Lucy ran into the bedroom and peered

out of the window. In the gloom of the trees she could just see the figure of a man walking back through the woods – a man wearing a dark jacket.

"Who was it?" Beth asked nervously. "Was it just a tramp?"

Lucy shook her head. "I don't know," she said. She shrugged. "I'd like to find out, but to tell you the truth, I'm more worried about that baby badger."

Chapter Four

Back at the farm, Lucy decided she wouldn't say anything to her mum or dad about going into the old cottage. She knew they'd be cross that she'd gone inside, and they might even forbid her from going down to the woods again – and she did want to go back and find out about the badgers.

Lucy checked on Rosie and the rest of the sheep in the paddock, and then went into the yard. Her dad had just shut the chickens up for the night and was trying to catch Bertram, their little red rooster, so he could be shut up safely too.

Bertram ran this way and that, tail feathers waving, squawking indignantly at being herded up with his hens, but at last Lucy cornered him, made a grab for him and popped him into the coop with the others.

"Well done," her dad said. "You're a lot quicker than I am."

Lucy was just about to start telling her dad about the baby badger when he beat her to it. "You had a bit of a wasted journey to Brockham Woods tonight, didn't you?" he said.

Lucy looked at him in astonishment. "How did you know that?" she asked and, before he could reply, added, "Well, yes we did, sort of. We only saw one baby badger."

He raised his eyebrows. "I'm surprised you even saw him."

"Why?" Lucy asked, puzzled. "How did you know they'd gone?"

"Because . . ." her dad said, "I'm afraid the badgers aren't there any more."

"What?" Lucy asked incredulously. "Why?"

Her dad hesitated. Two of the farm cats, thinking there was no one around, came out from the shelter of the hay barn and slid away into the shadows to catch an evening mouse or two.

"Because I'm afraid they've been . . . well, discouraged from living there."

"But *why*?"

"Look," her dad said, "I'm going to tell

you exactly what I heard at the Dog and Duck tonight. I dropped in for a pint and there was a group of farmers from over Honley way, talking about tuberculosis."

Lucy screwed up her face, confused. She knew that tuberculosis – or TB – was a disease which sometimes spread amongst a dairy herd. It was a terrible disease which could infect the cows' milk and occasionally spread to humans. "But what's that got to do with badgers?" she asked.

"Some people – not that I'm one of them – think that badgers can spread TB between herds. TB has been detected in a herd near Honley, and apparently there's a group of Honley farmers who have vowed to wipe out all badger setts within ten miles."

"No!" Lucy looked at her dad, horrified.

"They targeted Brockham Woods a couple of nights ago," her dad went on grimly. "Everyone knows about the huge old badger sett there."

Lucy gave a little cry.

"I'm sorry, love, but it looks as if your badgers have either been forced to move on elsewhere, or . . ."

Lucy stopped outside the kitchen window and buried her face in her hands. "*No!*" she cried. She couldn't bear to think that those lovely animals had been killed. "They can't have!"

Her dad looked sad. "I know it's awful, and I think it's wrong, but there it is. Some farmers just get fanatical about things."

"We waited for ages," Lucy said, shaking her head sadly. "I wondered where they'd all gone. I can't believe it. It's not fair!"

"I'm afraid that if farmers feel their livelihood is being threatened they tend to act first and think later," her dad said.

"How do they . . . what do the farmers do?" Lucy asked rather nervously.

"I'm not sure, love. To tell you the truth, I didn't ask. They either gas the badgers out, or fill up the holes so they can't get back into their living quarters."

"But what about the baby one I saw? D'you think he's all alone? How will he manage?"

"I'm sure he'll be all right. He'll either fend for himself or find another sett to live in," her dad said.

"Badgers don't do that!" Lucy said immediately. "They don't move between setts."

"Well, I don't know, love." Her dad shrugged. "I'm afraid you'll just have to forget about badgers. You've got all your animals here to look after. You can't look after every stray creature in the woods."

Lucy looked at her dad. *Oh, couldn't she?*

Lucy watched some TV with her parents and then she went over to the hay barn which adjoined the farm-house.

When Lucy's mum and dad had started doing Bed and Breakfast and they'd decided they needed Lucy's bedroom in the farmhouse for the guests, Lucy had been most upset. How awful, having to give up her big bedroom to total strangers! When they'd gone on to suggest, though, that the room upstairs in the old hay barn could be turned into a bedroom for her, she'd changed her mind. Now she loved her little room with its wooden floor, tiny windows and cosy red rug. One of the best things was that, because she had to climb a ladder and open a trapdoor to get into the room, Kerry couldn't get up there!

There was a low beam running through the room which had all Lucy's books along it, and before she went to sleep that night she went through all the wildlife ones. Eventually she found what she was looking for – details of Brocks, a sanctuary for badgers about twenty miles away. She'd ring them first thing in the morning, she decided, and find out what she could do for that baby badger.

If her dad thought she was just going to leave it there alone in the wood – well, he had another think coming!

Chapter Five

"Eclipse seems much calmer now," Lucy said to Giles, Major Steddington's manager. It was the following day, Saturday, and she was in Eclipse's stable, giving Donald a bit of a brush down.

"Yes, he is," Giles said, rather shortly. He'd come into the stable to check something on the racehorse's diet sheet. He looked at Lucy impatiently. "I'm afraid you're going to have to leave soon. We've got an important visitor coming – a man who may want the major to train his race-horses. The major wants all unnecessary people off the premises."

Lucy didn't say anything but, behind Donald, she made a face at Giles and carried on brushing. Giles, unaware he was being scowled at, noted something on his clipboard and went out.

Lucy straightened up and looked at the beautiful racehorse standing just behind them. "Do you like having my Donald here?" she asked softly. "Do you talk to each other?" She reached up to Eclipse and gently stroked the white diamond on the horse's head. "Do you have lots of horsey talks when the stable door's shut?"

Eclipse tossed his head slightly, but allowed himself to be stroked.

"You're beautiful, aren't you?" Lucy whispered. "The loveliest horse I've ever seen."

"Get away from that horse!" came a shout from outside, making Lucy jump. Rob, the stablehand, strode into the stable. "I've told you before, no one's to feed that horse except me."

"I was only stroking him," Lucy said, staring at Rob with dislike.

"Stroking him!" Rob exclaimed. "He's a racehorse, not a pet."

Lucy pursed her lips and finished grooming Donald without saying any more. It was only thanks to her and Donald, she thought, that Eclipse was far less nervous and more manageable now. And as if she'd ever do the slightest harm to any animal!

Taking her time, she finished grooming Donald and then went home. She was impatient to ring the badger sanctuary.

Some hours later, Lucy – with Beth and Courtney – was on her way to Brockham Woods.

"So badgers like peanuts, do they?" Beth asked, looking at the packet in Lucy's hand.

Lucy nodded. "Brocks – the sanctuary – said they're what badgers like best."

"I hope we see him," Courtney said, a whine in her voice. "I hope we haven't walked all this way for nothing."

Lucy shrugged. "I can't promise."

When she'd got home from the stud farm, Lucy had rung Brocks and told them about the baby badger. They'd told her to get some peanuts and put them outside the sett to see if that would lure him out. When, later that afternoon, Lucy had walked down to the village to buy a packet, she'd met up with Beth and Courtney. Beth had wanted to go down to the woods and see the baby badger again, and Courtney had said she wanted to come too. She'd complained steadily all the way, though – about the mud and the cold, and how she didn't even like the bluebells. Lucy was getting very fed up with her!

"Look, you've got to hide in there – behind that bush," Lucy said in a low voice when they got near the badger sett. The sun was just going down over the hill beyond, and the bluebell wood was dappled a soft pink. The recent rain had brought out the faint, beautiful scent of the flowers. Lucy thought it was all rather wonderful.

Courtney didn't agree. "Get down in the mud?" she asked, horrified. She looked down at herself – at her short tight skirt, leggings and silver and white trainers.

"That's right," Lucy said. "And please try not to make too much noise."

"Can't I just go and sit on the bank there?" Courtney asked.

Lucy shook her head. "This bush is a *hide* – you're supposed to hide from the animals you want to watch," she said. She carefully sprinkled the peanuts on the ground around the sett entrance where the baby badger had appeared before. Then she wriggled into the bush with Beth. "Come on," she said to Courtney. "You'd better get as comfortable as you can. We might have to wait for some time."

Courtney sighed loudly. "I hope it's not ages," she said. "I'm going to miss the new soap on TV. I wish I hadn't come now."

Lucy didn't say anything. She was wishing the same!

They waited fifteen minutes, and then Beth found some toffees in her pocket and shared them out. They were just settling down again when there was a slight rustling from the top of the bank.

"Quiet, everyone!" Lucy whispered.

Another minute or two went by with no noise at all and nothing to see, and then, just as before, the girls saw a little black snout appearing, followed by a black-and-white striped face.

"Ooh, is that him?" Courtney asked.

Lucy didn't reply, watching the little cub intently. The woman at the sanctuary had told her that if the badger actually began to eat, then he'd probably be able to fend for himself. If he didn't, then she was to ring Brocks again for more information. They'd be able to tell her what to do next.

"Aaah!" Courtney said. "Isn't he sweet?"

Lucy nudged her to be quiet. The little badger nosed around on the ground, sniffing at the peanuts, and then moved a bit further down the bank, snuffling around.

"He didn't eat any, did he?" Beth breathed.

Lucy shook her head worriedly.

The badger sniffed at a pile of damp leaves, then stood stock-still for a moment, looking small and lost and alone. He went back to the peanuts, moved past them again – and then Courtney sneezed. A very loud sneeze which seemed to echo right through the woods.

The badger disappeared in an instant.

Lucy turned to Courtney. "Why did you have to do that?" she seethed. "Couldn't you have put your hand over your nose or something?"

"Sorry!" Courtney said. She giggled. "I always do big loud sneezes. I can't help it!"

Lucy looked at Beth and sighed. "It didn't look as if he was going to eat anything, did it?"

Beth shook her head. "He looked quite thin, I thought. Thinner than last time."

"I'd better ring Brocks again," Lucy said. She got to her feet. "We might as well go home. He's not going to come out again now."

Courtney pulled a face. "Oh, sor-*rrry*!" she said sarcastically.

The girls walked back through the woods, Lucy wondering all the way what the sanctuary would say. As they approached the ruined cottage, she suddenly thought of something and stopped. "I wonder if that person who's staying in the cottage has anything to do with the group who harmed the badgers," she mused.

Beth tugged at her jacket. "Oh, come on! Don't let's go in there again. Let's just get past it quickly."

"Yeah, I'm cold," Courtney complained. She looked at her shoes. "And I'm covered in mud. I'm never going to get these trainers clean."

"Hang on a minute," Lucy said. She looked at the other two. "I'm not going to go inside – I just want to look through that downstairs window. You walk on slowly – I'll catch you up."

Leaving the other two on the path, Lucy approached the cottage, keeping under cover of the bushes in case there was anyone about.

Suddenly, when she was about two metres away, she heard the ring of a mobile phone. Lucy stopped dead. There *was* someone there – and it wasn't a tramp, either. Tramps didn't have mobile phones.

From inside the cottage she heard a man's voice. "Curtis. Yeah?"

Lucy couldn't see much, hidden behind a tangle of briars, but she could hear perfectly. The man speaking must be in the room downstairs.

"Tonight. One o'clock," she heard the man say, followed by a series of grunts of agreement. "I'll be there," he said eventually. "And the onward journey's all set up. I've emphasized that we have to do the deed before next month."

There was another pause and then he said, "It's an unmarked black van – OK, Giles? You just make sure the camera at the side gate is turned off."

Lucy froze. *Giles*!

"That creature won't see daylight again until it's in France. As long as old Stanley boy keeps out of the way we're home and dry."

There was another long silence. Carefully keeping under cover of the bushes, Lucy crept away to catch up with the others.

Was it the same Giles? The one at the stud farm? It wasn't exactly a common name. If it was, what on earth was going on?

Chapter Six

"But why did you go into the cottage any-way?" Lucy's mum asked crossly. "You must have known we wouldn't have allowed you to do that."

"I didn't go in there," Lucy said, cross-ing her fingers and thinking that it was true, she hadn't gone in *this* time. "I just stood outside and listened."

"Well, perhaps someone's bought the cottage and is about to have it done up," her mum said vaguely. "Perhaps they were just speaking to someone called Giles who's a builder."

Lucy shook her head. "I don't think so.

I'm sure it's something to do with the stud farm. Otherwise, why say that about turning off the camera?"

"I really don't know," said her mum. She hesitated, looking down at the big china dish in front of her on the pine kitchen table. "Now, have I already put tomato purée in there?"

Lucy sighed, twirling her hair round her finger. She was really quite bothered about what she'd overheard. She'd told Beth and Courtney, of course, but they hadn't been very interested, and by the time she'd arrived home her dad had gone out to a darts evening at the Dog and Duck, so she hadn't been able to tell him.

Lucy's mum had listened, of course, but she was more concerned about the fact that Lucy had been hanging around the cottage in the first place. Apart from that, she had a couple arriving at Hollybrook for bed, breakfast and evening meal the following week, and was busy trying to get three suppers cooked and frozen in advance.

"See what your dad says," Julie Tremayne said at last. "Let him decide whether to do anything about it."

"Can I wait up for him, then?" Lucy asked eagerly.

Her mum nodded. "I suppose so. Seeing as it's Sunday tomorrow. But he'll probably just think you've got your wires crossed somehow."

Lucy carried on twirling her hair, frowning. She had two problems – one was what she'd overheard at the cottage, and the other was the baby badger. By the time she'd got home, there had been no one at the Brocks office, so she'd left a message on their answerphone. She just hoped someone would ring her back before Monday – she was worried about how long it had been since the little badger had eaten anything.

"Now, seeing as I'm letting you stay

up," her mum said, "how would you like to help me make some pastry?"

Lucy pulled a face. "Do I have to?"

"There's a love. Go and get the plain flour out of the pantry for me, will you?"

Two hours later, Lucy was curled up in front of the TV, almost asleep. Her mum, after checking what programme Lucy was watching, had gone up to have a long bath, and Lucy had – for a special treat – let Roger and Podger come in from the boot lobby where they usually lived.

After bounding around the room madly, hardly able to believe their luck, both dogs had settled on the big shaggy rug in front of the sofa where Lucy lay. Now they were fast asleep, occasionally whimpering as they dreamed.

At ten-thirty there was the sound of the gate being opened, and a moment later Tim Tremayne's Land Rover pulled into the yard.

Lucy jumped up and stretched, waving to her dad from the window. The two dogs jumped up too, and went outside with her to meet him.

"What's this – a doorstep reception committee?" her dad asked. "Have you all come to see if I won the darts trophy?"

Lucy shook her head. "Mum said I could wait up and talk to you."

"What is it?" Tim Tremayne asked. He came into the lobby, patted the two dogs and made them get into their baskets. "There's nothing wrong with the herd, is there?"

Lucy shook her head. "No, nothing like that. It's just something funny I overheard." She was fully awake now. "It was while I was walking by the old cottage . . ." she began, and she told her dad everything – about what she'd heard the man on the phone saying, and how he'd used the name Giles. "I mean, Mum thinks there's nothing in it, but I was just a bit worried."

Her dad frowned. "It certainly seems strange," he said thoughtfully. "And there's no doubt that those horses are worth an absolute mint. There was a case a few years back – a valuable racehorse got stolen and was never seen again."

"So what good was it stealing him? If he was never seen again he couldn't race, could he?" Lucy said.

"They wanted to use him as a stud

horse," her dad explained. "They probably kept him on a farm somewhere secret and got him to father a great many new young racehorses. That's where the big, big money is."

"I see," Lucy said, nodding. So was *that* the reason someone was planning to steal a racehorse from Major Steddington's stables?

"But it all seems just a bit far-fetched really. We don't have that sort of thing happening round here. Though old Stanley Steddington ought to—"

"Stanley!" Lucy yelped.

Her dad looked at her in surprise. "What's the matter? That's the major's first name."

"It's what the man in the cottage said – *as long as old Stanley keeps out of the way* . . ."

"Are you sure he said that name?"

Lucy nodded excitedly. "Definitely!"

Her dad, who had sat down and was

just about to take his boots off, stood up again. "Come on then," he said.

"Where to?" Lucy asked, ready to rush out of the door immediately.

"I'm going to telephone Major Steddington and say we've got to see him urgently. It may be just a weird coincidence, but we'll let him decide that for himself."

"Fantastic!" Lucy said, and she dashed upstairs to tell her mum.

Chapter Seven

"I'm sorry, my dear. I'm not saying you're telling fibs or anything, I just think . . ." Major Steddington looked at Tim Tremayne. "Shall we . . . er . . . just say that some children have overactive imaginations?"

Lucy and her dad were in the major's comfortable study at the stud farm. The major had been very surprised to hear from Lucy's dad but had told them to come up to the stud immediately. When they arrived, he'd been doing some paperwork at his vast oak desk, but now he sat with them on a leather sofa in front of the fire.

"But they said about the camera . . ."
Lucy said urgently now. "And that a van
would be outside at one o'clock!"

"It sounds like a TV drama!" the major
said. He smiled at Lucy and brushed a hand
through his grey, wavy hair. "But I want to
thank you for coming, all the same."

"But he was speaking to someone called
Giles!" Lucy burst out.

"Giles is the son of an old friend of
mine, and he came to me with impeccable

70

references from his last employers," the major said, smiling. "I'd trust him with anything."

Tim Tremayne put his hand on Lucy's shoulder. "Come on, love," he said. "We'd better be off and get you to bed."

Lucy looked up at him, bitterly disappointed.

"Look, Lucy, the important thing is that we've told Major Steddington," her dad went on. "If he thinks everything's fine, then that's OK."

"And I must say I'm *very* pleased with your Donald," the major said. "Lovely temperament. Suits Eclipse very well."

Lucy racked her brains, looking round the room with its framed photographs of famous horses and their jockeys. She was perfectly sure now that what she'd overheard being planned *was* some sort of horse-theft. But how was she going to convince the major?

Brow furrowed, she tried hard to think

of some other detail – something she might have overlooked before. "He said something about having to have the job done before next month," she went on. "Aren't you having a new security system put in then?"

The major looked up at her in surprise. "Well, yes, we are," he said.

Suddenly Lucy remembered something else and clapped her hands in excitement. "When the man answered the phone he said, 'Curtis here'."

The major looked at her, puzzled. "Curtis?"

Lucy nodded vehemently.

"Are you sure it was *Curtis*?"

Lucy nodded again. The major looked thoughtful, drumming his fingers on the leather top of his desk.

"Does that name ring a bell with you, Major?" Lucy's dad asked.

The major frowned. "I'll say it does. I employed a man called Curtis until six months ago. He was my travelling head lad."

"But he doesn't work for you any more?"

"I sacked him because he was fiddling his transport allowance. He was jolly lucky I didn't get the police in."

"I bet it's him, then! I'm right!" Lucy burst out.

"I must admit he could be the sort of man who might hold a grudge against me," the major said, thinking hard. "And he would know the money that's involved . . ."

"Oh, do ring the police, Major!" Lucy implored. "Quickly! Before it's too late." She looked at her watch. "It's gone eleven o'clock now. That man said the van would be there at one o'clock!"

The major got to his feet. "You're right. I'll do it!" he said. "I'll do it right now."

*

As one o'clock drew near, Lucy and her dad were still in the major's study. He and Tim Tremayne had decided it was safer that they should stay there, unseen. Lucy was very relieved – she would have hated to have gone home and missed everything!

In the major's study, fixed to the wall, were three television screens linked to the three cameras set on the walls around the stud. The first showed a general view of the large courtyard, the second was of the side entrance and the third covered the main gate.

The police had been called and were outside the stud, down the road in a red van marked GAS EMERGENCY REPAIRS. Two more policemen were actually on the premises. They had been let in the tradesmen's entrance wearing plain clothes and were now concealed somewhere in the stables. Major Steddington, having thought things through properly, was now certain that it was Eclipse who was going to be snatched. He'd told Lucy and her dad that Eclipse was probably the most famous, and certainly the most expensive, horse that they'd ever had.

"Now I've started to think about it, everything adds up," the major said, coming in just before one o'clock to report on what was happening. Lucy exchanged a gleeful glance with her dad. "The cameras are notoriously unreliable – that's why the new system is being installed – so if one goes blank no one thinks anything of it. Two of my stablehands are on holiday so we're short-staffed, and one o'clock is the changeover time for the security guard." He gave a wry smile. "And guess who's on duty from midnight until six a.m.?"

"Giles!" Lucy guessed.

The major nodded. "The very one." He glanced at his watch. "Nearly time. I'd better be getting back. I've been told to do

75

my usual night-time round of the horses, just as I normally would."

As the door closed behind him, Lucy turned to her dad. "Oh, can't we go and see what's going on?" she said longingly.

"Of course we can't!" Tim Tremayne said. "You don't want anyone involved to realize that you were responsible for tipping off the major, do you?"

Lucy sighed. "I suppose not."

Her dad pointed to the nearest TV screen. "Look, there's the major."

Lucy looked at the TV intently. "Who's that with him?"

"That's one of the policemen," her dad said. He chuckled. "They've put a green padded jacket and flat cap on him so that he looks like a stablehand."

Suddenly, as Lucy was watching the major and the policeman walk across the yard, the second screen went blank. She gave an excited squeal. "It's happening!

Someone's turned the side-gate camera off."

"So they have!" her dad said.

They looked at the other two screens. On the first one the major and the policeman had gone out of view, and the courtyard with its tubs of flowers was empty. The third showed the front entrance, which was completely quiet.

"What d'you think's happening?" Lucy said urgently.

Her dad raised his eyebrows. "How about if we creep down the passage and look out of the end window?"

"Ooh yes!" Lucy said.

Putting his finger to his lips, Tim Tremayne silently opened the door of the study, and the two of them crept down to the end of the hall, where there was a window which overlooked the side gate.

"Keep back so you won't be seen," her dad ordered.

Heart pounding with excitement, Lucy

did as she was told, pressing herself back into the darkness. For a few moments all was quiet – and then, suddenly, there was a faint thudding noise from across the courtyard.

"Something's happening!" Lucy breathed. Next moment, the shadowy figure of a man leading a horse came into view. The horse's feet had been wrapped with some sort of soft cloth so they wouldn't make a noise on the cobblestones, but even in the semi-darkness Lucy could pick out the white diamond on the horse's forehead.

"That's Eclipse!" she whispered excitedly.

The man led Eclipse to the side-gate, got out a key and opened it – and then, suddenly, two great arc lights were turned on, temporarily blinding the man and making the horse shy and whinny with fright.

"It's Giles!" Lucy said in a breathless whisper, able to see the man leading the horse clearly for the first time.

As the side-gate swung open, Lucy could just see a large black horsebox parked in the roadway. There seemed to be two men in the front. Lucy pointed them out to her dad. "I wonder if one of them is Curtis?"

Before her dad could reply, the men had leaped out of the horsebox and were running down the lane. Lucy heard the sound of slamming car doors and the pounding of feet as six policemen raced from a red van. After some shouting and scuffling, two of them caught and overpowered the men from the horsebox. Two more police-men went round to the back of the van – perhaps to see if there were any other gang members inside, Lucy thought.

She watched breathlessly as the two other policemen moved swiftly towards Giles, who was still standing fixed and immobile under the lights as if he was too stunned to move.

One of the policemen – used to horses, Lucy thought – soothed the nervous Eclipse and then took the halter rope from Giles. She heard Giles say something to him, something clipped and bitter, but the policeman didn't reply. The other police-man spoke, though. Lucy wondered if he was saying what they always said on television – about Giles not having to say anything, but anything he did say might be taken in evidence . . .

As a police car drew up across the stable

entrance, the major appeared out of the shadows with Rob, his stablehand. Lucy heard the major shout something at Giles, and it seemed as if he wanted to go up and confront him, but Rob grabbed the major's arm, holding him back. Rob then took the horse's reins from the policeman, and he and the major waited there, talking soothingly to Eclipse, as handcuffs were clapped on Giles and he was led into the back of the police car.

Lucy watched the scene unfold before her, her heart pounding.

"Oh, wow!" she said as the yard slowly cleared of people. "What a night." Suddenly she felt incredibly tired, as if she'd just run a long race.

Her dad tousled her hair. "Well, they've caught the men and Eclipse is safe, love," he said. "Well done! Very well done!"

Chapter Eight

"Well done, indeed!" Major Steddington said, clapping Lucy on the shoulder. "If it hadn't been for you nosing about that old cottage, we might never have found out what was being planned."

Lucy smiled at him across their kitchen table. She was thrilled the men had been caught, of course, but it was Sunday morning now, she'd heard from the badger sanctuary and was anxious to get down to Brockham Woods again. "That's all right," she said politely.

"Curtis had been using that cottage as his base for some days while he organized the van and made his final arrangements for Eclipse to be hidden."

"We're just pleased it all worked out," Lucy's mum said, refilling the major's coffee cup.

The major thanked her, then reached under the table and brought out a large carrier bag. "I've bought you this as a thank you, Lucy," he said. "It's something for that nice little donkey of yours."

Lucy opened the bag and pulled out a smart red head collar. "Oh, it's lovely!" she said, thrilled. "Donald will look great in it."

The major nodded. "He should be back with you in a month or two. We're going to get a couple of donkeys of our own, you see. Now that I've seen Donald with Eclipse – well, a donkey is just what a restless racehorse needs."

"A slice of bread pudding, Major?" Lucy's mum asked.

"Don't mind if I do," said Major Steddington comfortably.

Lucy wriggled in her seat. "Can I go now?" she said. "I want to go and see how my badger is."

"Course you can," her mum said.

Lucy thanked the major again and then dashed over to the hay barn and climbed the ladder to her room. She took what was left of the packet of peanuts, plus a thick old jumper, and then, in one of the sheds in the yard, found the small carrying basket they sometimes used to take a cat or bird to the vet.

The woman at Brocks had told Lucy that as the little badger hadn't immediately started eating, he could have still been feeding from his mother at the time she'd disappeared, and may not have been taught how to forage in the ground for worms and bugs. She'd told Lucy to try and catch the badger, and then give them a call so they could come and collect him. He'd need bottle-feeding until they could release him back into the wild.

"I could bottle-feed him," Lucy had said eagerly, remembering how she'd raised Rosie the lamb.

But the woman at Brocks hadn't been too keen on that, saying that there was a very specific milk mixture to use, and besides, badgers – however cute – shouldn't be treated as pets. "He'll have to go back into the wild as soon as possible, and if he gets too used to humans he'll find it difficult to adjust." She'd said that if Lucy couldn't manage to catch the badger, then someone from Brocks would come over.

But Lucy was determined to have a try herself! Armed with the things she'd collected, she set off for Brockham Woods.

Lucy had been in the hide for about an hour, listening and watching the spot on the bank where the little badger had previously appeared and where she'd spread the rest of the peanuts. All the nuts she'd left there a day or so earlier had gone, but

Lucy knew that this could be because squirrels, mice or birds had taken them. Her badger might not have had anything at all to eat since the sett had been disturbed.

She strained her eyes once more – were those bluebells swaying because of the wind, or was there a small animal moving about? Silently, she moved a branch out of her view in order to see better. Yes! It *was* the little badger.

Keeping absolutely still, Lucy watched him move right down the bank and almost onto the path. Every so often his black snout would lift into the air to sniff, but luckily the breeze was blowing Lucy's scent away from him, so he didn't detect anything to make him nervous. He sniffed around the nuts but seemed to push them aside – at least, Lucy didn't notice him chewing. He came closer and closer to her and Lucy hardly breathed. The woman at Brocks had told her to try and get between the badger and his hole, so that he couldn't run back into it.

He came closer still. Lucy waited . . . and then, all of a sudden, she lunged forward out of the bush and dropped her thick jumper straight onto the cub.

"Got you!" she said. "Got you, little Snouty."

She picked him up, jumper and all, for the woman had told her that even a small badger might give a nasty bite, and dropped him into the basket. Snouty, as Lucy had named him, made a faint mewing sound, like a kitten.

"It's not for long," Lucy said to him, delighted that her plan had gone so smoothly. "The nice Brocks woman will come and get you and look after you properly."

Two hours later, back at Hollybrook, a green and white van with BROCKS written on the side pulled into the yard.

Lucy ran out to greet the woman driver and introduce herself. "I've put Snouty in the hay barn," she said, pointing. "He's out of reach of the dogs there. They got a bit too interested in him."

The woman patted her on the shoulder. "Well done you for catching him," she said. "We'll look after him from now on."

"You heard about what happened at the big old sett in the woods? I don't know exactly what the farmers did, but there's no badgers left there any more."

The woman shook her head sadly. "I know and I'm desperately sorry," she said. "The only consolation is that often badgers will move into another sett on a temporary basis, and then move back to their original one when they think it's safe. It could be that we can take this little chap back home in a couple of months' time."

Lucy pushed open the door of the hay barn and nodded towards the basket. "There's Snouty!"

They both peered through the openings in the tough plastic cage. Snouty was lying sleek and flat along one edge, half-hidden under some straw. "He looks a fine little chap," the woman said. "Well done!"

"I wish I could keep him," Lucy said wistfully.

The woman laughed. "Badgers don't

make very good pets, unfortunately. They're a lot more fierce than they look." She carried the basket to the van and deftly transferred the badger into a steel cage.

"Would you like to do one more thing for him?" she asked Lucy.

Lucy nodded eagerly.

"I've bought a bottle of milk mixture. Would you like to give it to him?"

"Yes, please!" Lucy said. She took the bottle from the woman and, bending down to the cage, held the bottle through the bars and let the baby badger suck from it.

"Just as I thought," the woman said. "He's starving!"

Snouty took just a couple of minutes to drink all that was in the bottle. Then he curled round in a ball like a cat, and went to sleep.

"He's lovely, isn't he?" Lucy sighed.

"Yes, he is – and you've saved him," the woman said. "He wouldn't have survived if you hadn't found him."

"Well, that's evens, then," Lucy said, "because it was only through *him* that a racehorse got saved."

The woman laughed as she got into the van. "D'you know," she said. "For a moment there, I thought you said he saved a racehorse."

"I did!" Lucy said, but the woman had driven away by then, still laughing.

Lucy made her way back into the hay barn, thinking that as Snouty was gone, she'd just have to make do with Rosie and Donald and the rest of the farm animals. At least, until the next animal adventure came along!